HOLLY'S JOY

A NOVELLA

SHEILA MURDOCK

ALSO BY SHEILA MURDOCK

DIVESTED
Crystal
THE DIVESTED BWWM SERIES
SHEILA MURDOCK
The Vain Society
SHEILA MURDOCK
Entitled Women
SHEILA MURDOCK
LAVONNE ON THE JOB
The Hair Salon
SHEILA MURDOCK
HIS Mess HIS Stress
A NOVEL
SHEILA MURDOCK
LESSONS Lisa
THE LESSONS SERIES
SHEILA MURDOCK
Billionaire Bliss
SHEILA MURDOCK
ATTEND AT YOUR OWN RISK
THE Club
A NOVEL
SHEILA MURDOCK
STANDALONES and STANDALONE SERIES
MORE to COME!

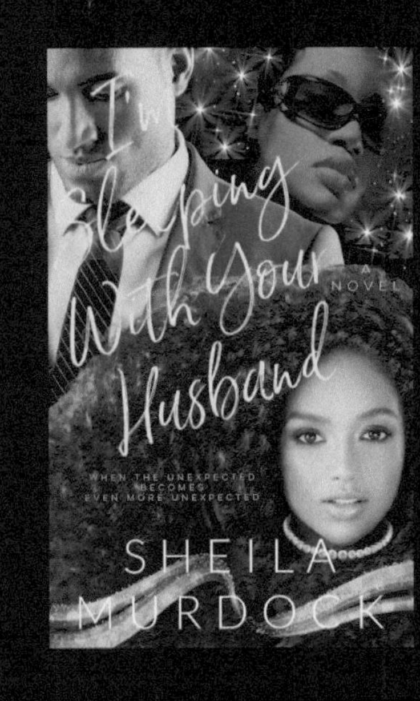

STANDALONES

MORE to COME!

THOUGHT - PROVOKING
SHORT STORIES
IT'S NOT ALWAYS A BAD THING
Passed UP
A SHORT STORY
SHEILA MURDOCK
IT'S NOT ALWAYS A BAD THING
Gave UP
A SHORT STORY
SHEILA MURDOCK
IT'S NOT ALWAYS A BAD THING
Meet UP
A SHORT STORY
SHEILA MURDOCK
MORE to COME!

NIGHT SKY
AFFAIR

LILA CYNTHIA PAMELA TABITHA

short story series

MORE to COME!

NIGHT SKY AFFAIR - TABITHA - COMING IN 2025

THE LOVELLA NOVELLA FOR ANY TIME OF THE YEAR

MORE to COME!

HOLLY and RUDY - COMING SOON

NEW HOLIDAY NOVELLA FOR ANY TIME OF THE YEAR

MORE to COME!

He broke her heart. She broke his. They remained friends. And they haven't seen each other in 20 years.

Once divided now reunited, she wants to rekindle what was lost in the past. A past that was uncertain, a past full of unforgettable memories. A past full of heartache.

A past that should've perhaps stayed where it was . . . in the past.

Aiden Crawley clearly moved on and doesn't believe in starting over. But when he sees Shanna Flanders after a 20-year hiatus, he can't deny the crashing wave of feelings that come over him.

But everything that starts eventually comes to an end, but not in the way either one of them will ever expect.

When wanting to rekindle a long-in-the-past romance becomes a mystery no one ever saw coming, it will be one that one of them will never, ever forget.

WHERE THINGS END - COMING IN 2025

CONTENTS

1
THE JOY OF CHOICES

I didn't wanna go to this party tonight. I really didn't. After such a disappointing year and seeing everyone celebrate all yearlong with the things in life that they should be celebrating about—like my brother finally getting married to his high-school sweetheart and my other married sister having her first baby, while my other sister—who is five years younger than me—just celebrated her one-year wedding anniversary. And my *other* sister—who is the oldest of us five—just opened up her law firm while raising four boys. She's married, too. I felt like I was being left behind—again . . . and again . . . and again. And that was just within my family. I didn't wanna get into friends and ex-boyfriends.

Whatever joy I had left in me had pretty much dissipated—wiped clean because of envy, even though people just didn't think I had the right to envy anyone because of my lifestyle. Yeah, I may be the one percent of the one percent, but that didn't mean my life was always fabulous. I'm human above everything. I have feelings above everything, and not being able to share them with someone I felt they were worth sharing with was just about pushing me to the breaking point; made me feel like rolling up a joint, and I didn't even smoke, but the past Christmas years I had were a complete joke.

But my mom didn't joke when it came to her Midnight Christmas Wishes party. But I wished she didn't have it this year. It was the one thing she always looked forward to every year, and if one got an invite to it, they felt like they were the most privileged person in this world. But it always appeared to me that the same people attended it every year, even though my parents—especially my mom—claimed they didn't run a closed circle of friends and family. They were the ones everyone seemed to have wanted to be, and they expected perfection from their children—no exceptions. They loved showing us off at this party every year, and that's another reason I didn't feel like going. I didn't have a good year, but she didn't seem to care at all about that, just that I showed up in an Oscar de la Renta or Monique Lhuillier dress, but this was more of a casual formal party, not a Christmas gala—but they had one of those just two weeks prior. I was tired of a life of constant flashy parties where everyone just showed up to gossip and talk about who had on the best or worst attire, amongst other things. Everyone was so fake, I mean, really. But the only thing that wasn't fake was the level of wealth and all of the money, and being in this lifestyle my whole life gave me the gift of access to seeing things most didn't see. I saw way too much of things that were clearly bought, from spouses to whatever a person could imagine. I should not have seen a lot of things until I was ready, and I'd just turned 30.

I felt the best—and worst—was yet to come.

But I couldn't pay my way out of not being there tonight, so I'd been rummaging through my closet trying to figure out what I wanted to wear while also trying to figure out how I was gonna wear a smile on my face all night—and I was blessed enough to have an endless number of options. Since this party started right at midnight on Christmas day, I still had a few hours to get ready for it, but if I was a minute late, I was gonna be left out in the cold, literally. My dad didn't care at all about being on time, but being on time to their party meant everything to my mom. In Christmas years past, I'd seen her have her security men turn people away just for being just a few minutes late. She didn't wanna hear any excuses. She said it was disrespectful and an insult to the Harper family for not showing up at *her* party on time.

Those people were automatically blacklisted from invitations to any more of our family parties in the future, and my mom made sure of it. And, of course, in her classic bully fashion, she said that included her children as well because we should've known better most of all.

My phone rang.

I looked to see who it was and it was a FaceTime call from my sister Hyacinth—the one named after a flower, as well as the one who had her first child—my niece—this year. "Hi, Hy."

"Hey, Holly. I just wanted to check on you to make sure you were leaving now to the party?" she asked, as she held my six-month-old niece in her arms while she had her bundled up and ready to go.

"Why the hell are all of you leaving so early?" I checked my watch. "We have now two hours to get to the party."

"Mom wants everyone there early this year because she doesn't want people getting there right before midnight like what they've done in the past, and you know they're pushing it more and more with how they're arriving right at the cut-off time."

"Um, it is a midnight party that starts at midnight."

She sighed. "Holly, *you know* not to argue with her. This is her thing more than it is Dad's. You know to get there early because you don't wanna hear her mouth if we don't. She told me that people are looking forward to seeing the baby."

"Yeah, and she's your and Chris's baby, not mine. No one is looking forward to seeing me, Hy. I just wanna stay home this year to tell you the truth."

"Holly, you know you can't do that. Everyone does look forward to seeing you. It's one of the only few days of the year that we're all together in the same house. You know you have to be there and remember you have to wear a dress or skirt like every year."

I rolled my eyes. "I know, Hy. I don't need a lecture. You think just because you became a mom this year you wanna start sounding like Mom. I don't need it, okay? I know what to wear and what not to wear."

"I know, Holly. And you know we all want you to have a better year next year than you've had this year. Maybe this can be the night that you can forget about everything that'd happened this year and already get a great start for next year. Maybe you'll meet your future husband there."

"You all say that crap every year, Hy. I'm not meeting anyone new there tonight. Mom still thinks she can get me with Vester Wayland. *Everyone knows* about him except his parents, but I honestly think they do know, they're just in some serious denial."

She laughed. "Yeah, I think they are, too. And our mom is as well."

"Yeah, that's why I don't feel like having the little joy left in me for this year completely wiped away by sitting there talking to a man that no woman in this world has any chance with whatsoever."

"Yeah, don't waste your time, Holly. But I did ask Mom and she told me there should be some single new men there for you to meet."

"I'll believe it when I see them."

She sighed. "Well, Chris is ready to go. You know we live a half hour away so that's why we're leaving right now. And, Holly, I suggest you figure out what you're gonna wear fast because you don't wanna be late because you know what's gonna happen if you are."

"She's not leaving anyone out in the damn cold, Hy, especially one of her own children. She's made those threats every year since we've been living on our own."

"And she hasn't had to make good on them yet because we've always been there on time. She just likes to remind us, that's all."

"Well, whatever. I'll get there when I get there, but I will get there before midnight."

"Fine, suit yourself," she said, as they walked out into their garage to their Lamborghini Urus SUV. "Just call me when you're about to leave because I wanna see what you're wearing."

"Fine, bye."

"Bye, Holly."

I went back to rummaging through my closet which was in a different room from my bedroom. Although I had an endless number of options, I just didn't feel like wearing a dress. I even thought about showing up in an evil elf's outfit to protest what I always had to wear at these parties. Yeah, I knew I'd be the talk then!

I continued to sift through my closet and came up on a beautiful pair of Dolce&Gabbana yellow pants embellished in chunky, sparkling colorful crystals all over them. I just remembered I'd bought them to wear to a friend's Christmas party at a club a few weeks ago but decided to wear something else. I pulled them out and grinned at the $5,540 price tag. I didn't want a pricy pair of pants like these go unworn, plus, they were very festive and instantly brightened my mood and got me more into the Christmas spirit. I decided to wear them along with a $3,998 Herve L. Leroux sleeveless peplum white top that I'd never worn. I started to see just how many pieces of clothes I had that had these price tags still attached to them, and there were people out there struggling to pay their bills and barely able to stay in their homes, and here I was living by myself in a house my parents bought for me that cost in the millions. I had a lot to rethink about how I looked at things, but I wasn't able to do that tonight because I had to get to a party where everyone thought was gonna be the best thing that was gonna happen this year—and maybe it was to them—but I had other things on my mind, but I had to put it all to the side for a party I just didn't feel like going to.

I looked at the time—still two hours to go. I felt like time was standing still. I went to my shoe shelf and looked for a pair of shoes to complement my outfit, and any color would do, but I decided to go for the Rene Caovilla Transmission ivory/white 105mm heel sandals with gorgeous sparkling clear crystals and a super silver glittery outsole. These shoes were also brand new and never worn since I had them in a variety of different colors. I guess I was really trying to get into a more joyous, holiday spirit with a bright and super blingy holiday look for this year's party, a look my mom would gasp in complete disapproval of—and I couldn't wait to see her face when she did!

I sat down at my vanity set and got my makeup look together, and thought I had a bit of talent in this beauty department since I could put beautiful makeup looks together with everything I wore and didn't look like Bozo the Clown when I was done. It was, after all, how my mom met my dad well over 45 years ago when she was working at a makeup counter in a luxury department store. He said it was love at first sight when he saw her, they got married a year later, and the rest, as they say, is history.

But I wanted to build my own history with someone, and I just didn't think I was gonna find him at these parties my parents threw each year, especially this one. I knew that was what my mom had always hoped for—much more than my dad did—but I felt that if it didn't happen by now then it was never going to and that was fine with me.

After I was done getting my makeup look together, I took a look at my hair since my mom thought I had the most beautiful hair out of my sisters, and she always wanted me to wear it down so she could thoughtlessly brag to other women how super long and beautiful it was and especially most of all loved to stress that it was "all mine." I felt I was 10 years old—not 30 years old—when she did this. I was wearing it up in a huge bun on the top of my head tonight.

I looked at the time. It was now less than two hours to get to the party, but I felt I still had plenty of time since after all, I only lived 5 miles away from them. I was in no rush at all. I went to my coat closet and pulled out a beautiful Giorgio Armani green leather coat with snap buttons and a detachable tall shearling collar. At $13,000, it was about time and definitely cold enough for me to wear it. As I tried it on to see how it would look, I got another FaceTime call, this time from my other big sister Hannah, who was the oldest of us five. "Hannah, what's up?"

"Holly? Are you ready to leave?" she asked, as she stared at me like she couldn't believe what I had on.

"Yeah, in probably about another hour."

"Holly . . ."

"Hannah, please, okay? Hy was trying to talk me into leaving early so I wouldn't be late, so don't you start it, too. You know I'm only five miles away so I'm not in any rush to get there, but apparently you were since you're already there as I can see."

"Most of the guests are already here, Holly. Let me see what you're wearing," she said, as I could see she was all decked out in one of the latest Oscar de la Renta holiday dresses.

I stood back so she could check out what I would be decking my parents' halls in for this year.

She gasped! "Holly! You *can't* be serious! *That's* what you're wearing here?"

"Yeah, and why not? It's a festive holiday look," I said with a slight grin.

"You know Mom is *not* gonna approve of that. You look like you're going to a rapper's Christmas party."

"Been to a ton them," I replied with an even bigger grin. "Public and private ones."

"Holly, I suggest you change. You have a little time since you're not far away from here at all. Like I said, Mom is not gonna like it if you show up with that on."

"Well, that's too bad because I already have it on. See you when I get there."

"Holly! I have to tell—"

I hung up and went back to my bedroom while laughing since I actually could not wait to see the looks on everyone's faces, especially Mom's, and I knew there weren't gonna be any different than Hannah's!

It was now an hour before the party really got started. I decided I would get there early since I was already dressed. I put on my coat and grabbed my Hermes Birkin 25 red crocodile bag—a past Christmas gift. I took a selfie in the mirror of my foyer for my social media pages. I laughed as I looked like I had a furry neck collar on and headed to my garage where one of my cars waited for me, my silver Bentley Bentayga SUV, something I bought when my boyfriend broke up with me for a racially ambiguous IG thot. I was really trying to make myself feel good this year, but materialism only lasts for as long as it will last, and the lasting effect of it with these gifts had worn off completely. I pressed the button on my home phone app and the garage lifted up . . . to a blizzard wonderland.

The forecast said nothing about snow tonight.

2
THE JOY OF ENTITLEMENT

As I pulled out of my garage and on to my heated driveway, I received another FaceTime call.

Hannah.

Again.

"Hannah, what's up?"

"Holly, I hope you're leaving now."

"Yes, I'm leaving right now. Did you know it was gonna be like this?"

"Yeah, they changed the forecast about two hours ago and said a storm was rolling in. That's what I was trying to tell you before you hung up on me the last time I called you."

"Oh, okay. Sorry I did that. I haven't been looking out the window and have had all of my blinds shut since it's dark out. I didn't know it was gonna be this bad. The last time I looked at the forecast it didn't mention anything about a storm coming. I know if they did then Mom would've cancelled the party."

"Yeah, she probably would've because it's getting bad out there."

"*Getting bad*? It already is!" I said, as I drove off onto the road where it appeared that they only plowed it once so far.

"Look, take your time getting here, okay? Hy and Chris just got here with the baby because they were slowed down a lot because of the weather since they live a half hour away. You're the only one who lives the closest to here, but you know how much longer it can take."

"Yeah, I know, Hannah. I can barely see ahead of me so I need to get off of this phone so I can concentrate on the road. You know how different everything looks when it snows and especially when it snows like this and especially at night."

"Okay, Holly. Please be careful. Mom even told me that it doesn't matter what time you get here now, as long as you get here safely."

"Thank y'all for thinking of me."

She sighed. "Holly, *be careful*."

Minutes later, the snow still hadn't let up. It was just coming down at a faster and heavier pace. Normally I would say that it looked beautiful, but there was nothing beautiful about driving in it. I admit now that I should've left earlier when it wasn't nearly this bad. This is also what I get for not keeping up with the changes in the weather especially this time of the year, but especially for tonight. I knew better than this. I'd been caught on the road when it snowed more than once, but had never been caught in anything like this.

I was now going at a snail's pace as I saw cars spun out everywhere in the middle of the road as well as in ditches. With my windshield wipers on full speed, I could only see the blur of colorful Christmas lights and decorations and I wished they could guide me safely to my parents' house. Five miles in this mess seemed like fifty, but I felt a little relaxed in the fact that my mom wanted me to take my time getting there, and that's exactly what I was gonna do because I had no choice. I hated driving in this weather; I hated it ever since I was in college. I didn't mind in high school because I was excited about driving, but now the thrill had been gone for very long, and I didn't wanna be out in it unless I absolutely had to, and my parents' party was —according to them and tradition—an absolutely had to.

"This storm is not letting up," I mumbled to myself as I only seemed to have been going no more than 5 miles-per-hour—might as well have put it in neutral—and I wasn't moving any faster for anyone. Even in the best conditions, people usually kept their distance behind me when I was driving this Bentley, so I guess in a lot of ways I didn't have to worry about someone being too close to me. I looked in my rearview mirror almost every second, more than what was required for typical driving. Driving in this may have been typical, but it was typical on a whole other level.

A snowplow blew past me!

I screamed from being startled at it but calmed myself down. I slowly merged into the lane of the snowplow since it was a little less snow-covered than the one I was in, but I knew I still had to take it easy. I turned on John Legend's "Silver Bells" to get me more in an upbeat mood during this drive because it was gonna take me even longer than I thought to get there. Out of nowhere, I started to laugh about a Christmas in the past:

Christmas Eve, 10 Years Ago

"Well, you know we have only an hour to get to my parents' Midnight Wishes Christmas party, so I'm glad we decided to open our gifts here. I'm glad you like your gift."

"Love it," Marwell replied, as he looked at his Rolex watch. "As a professional athlete, people think we're some spoiled guys who get whatever we want. Some were even saying that I was using you because you're from the Harper family. Everyone knows your family are billionaires."

"And it took decades for us to get to where we are. I'm only 20 years old and live in this beautiful house all by myself. My younger sister Hollis is gonna move in once she's 18 so I won't be that lonely around here."

"It's great that the two of you get along," he said with a smile.

"We do," I said, as I was getting a little anxious for my gift. "So, where's *my* gift?" I guess I just couldn't hide it.

He smiled and went behind the tree and got a huge box out from underneath it. "Here you go, baby. Merry Christmas."

"Oooooh! I think I know what this is! Merry Christmas!" I said as I tore off the wrapping and saw it was from one of my favorite designers—Louis Vuitton. "Louis! Louis!"

He laughed. "Yeah, I think you already know what it is."

"Oh, yes! I think I know, too!" I opened this huge box and shrieked in excitement when I saw my gift in its dustcover. I knew by the shape of it that it was exactly what I wanted. I smiled big at him as he smiled back at me. I pulled down the cover so fast I thought I ripped it . . . .

To a hat box.

I gave him a more-than-disappointed look.

"What? What's the matter? That's the one you said you wanted, right? A hat box."

I gave a loud, disappointing sigh. "Marwell. I already have this hat box. I have both sizes. This is *not* the hat box I was talking about that I wanted."

"What? Are you serious, Holly?"

"Does it look like I'm kidding?" I said as I narrowed my eyes on him.

"Don't look at me like that," he warned. "You told me you wanted a hat box."

"I WANTED THE *CROCODILE* HAT BOX! THE ORANGE

ONE WITH THE JEWELED ORNAMENT ON THE HANDLE! THIS IS THE CLASSIC MONOGRAM! I ALREADY HAVE 2 PIECES LIKE THIS!"

"Lower your voice right now. There's no reason to yell."

"Yeah, well, I can yell as much as I damn well want to because this is my house! And how the hell do you think I'm gonna act when I told you I wanted the orange crocodile hat box from the fall/winter runway show, and you got me something I already have?!"

"You don't wear that many hats anyway, only when you go on vacation."

"That's not the point!" I got up as I shook my head as I walked to the window to try my best to calm myself down.

He got up and stood right by me. "Look, if you wanna know the truth, Holly, I couldn't afford to get you that particular one, okay? It was too expensive. I'm not one of the highest paid players in my profession—not even close—you know that."

"Then you misrepresented yourself. You misrepresented yourself to me and my family."

"I did nothing like that at all, Holly, and you know it! Now you're talking crazy just because I couldn't afford to get you something you really wanted. And I'm sorry I got you something you already have. You have so many bags and luggage and travel pieces that I honestly didn't know you already had all of the sizes they make for this item—you should've told me."

"I shouldn't have had to tell you, Marwell. You should've got me exactly what I wanted. Rick definitely would've," I said, since Rick was my boyfriend in high school.

"And just what the hell does your ex-boyfriend from high school have to do with this?"

"None of your business! But I sure as hell got you what you wanted; something you clearly couldn't afford to get yourself."

"Now you watch it! I mean it! I'll gladly take the gift back if you don't want it and get something for myself if that's the way you wanna be about this. I wasn't gonna go broke getting you something for Christmas that you would probably forget and would be in the back of your closet."

"I was planning on taking it on my trip to Maldives with my friends next month, *if* you got me the right item. Are you really that broke?"

He let out a sarcastic laugh. "I don't get paid like the way you thought I did, Holly. I'm one of the lowest paid players in my profession, okay?"

"So you *do* only wanna be with me for my money, huh? That's what my friends and family said."

"And you believe everything they tell you?"

"Well, I believe this! And you telling me you couldn't afford to get me what I really wanted proves they were right!"

He shook his head with a sigh. "Do you want the gift or not?"

"Is that a trick question?"

"No, it's a serious question," he replied with a daunting glare in his eyes.

"I don't want something I already have."

"And that's fine and I understand," he said, and picked up the hat box, put it back in its dustcover, and put it back in the box it came in. He sat back down as he shook his head. "What the hell is wrong with you, Holly?"

"What the hell is wrong with you for not getting me what I wanted this Christmas?"

"Don't answer a question with a question. But if you wanna play that game then fine. I'm now glad I didn't get you what you really wanted, Holly. For once, I put myself and my finances first. You're nothing but an entitled little monster who was born like this. All you care about is material shit, and why wouldn't you? You grew up in a family who can afford to get you anything you want without you ever having to lift a finger to do anything worth doing, like having a job and earning your own living and taking care of yourself. But I thought I saw something more in you, Holly, when we met. I thought you weren't like all of the other materialistic rich chicks out there."

"I'm not!" I hissed.

"You're right, you're not. You're worse."

I gasped! "Take that back!"

"The only thing I'm taking back is this gift. And it's going right back to the store." He took off the brand-new Rolex watch I'd just given him. "Oh, and you can take this back to the store you got it from as well." He stood up and put it on the chair he was sitting on. "I don't need anything from you anymore, Holly. This is it. You ruined my Christmas with your baby bullshit; wiped all of my joy right out of me."

"*Your* joy? I just wiped all of the joy out of you, huh? What the hell about *my* joy, Marwell? I just got all of mine wiped out as well! Your feelings aren't the only ones that matter."

"I never said they did, Holly, but all you care about is your feelings, not mine or anyone else's. You've proven that tonight, and you've proven that you've just been a complete asshole throughout our relationship, all 9 months of it—you know *that* as well. And as long as you live this way then you're always gonna be this way. I really feel sorry for you."

He walked towards the door with the box in his hands as Mariah Carey's "All I Want For Christmas Is You" played on the speakers throughout the room.

"Wait! Where are you going? We have the party to go to!"

"Are you kidding me? I'm going home. We're through, Holly, so ask Rick to take you since he can afford to buy you exotic gifts, you Silver Bells bitch! Merry Christmas!"

"Silver Bells bitch," I said with a full grin. I broke out into a full laugh. This was what people called rich girls during the holiday season, and I was called it a lot—and still was. "Well, he was right. I was very young back then but hardly changed at all in the ten years since he'd ended our relationship." I was talking out loud as if someone else was in here with me, but I did this during bad weather because it calmed my nerves, but this was some of the worst weather I'd ever driven in. I felt like I was only inching along and knew it was gonna be way past midnight before I got to my parents' house for the party.

Marwell was the best boyfriend I'd had in the ten years since he'd broken up with me on Christmas Eve, right before we were supposed to go to the party, all over a gift that I already had that he didn't know I had. Looking back, I thought that was very nice of him—as well as very honest—to tell me the real reason why he didn't get me what I really wanted, even though I could afford to get it myself. I didn't handle myself that well at all, and it got out everywhere on social media since it was in its infancy back then about the way I acted on that day. But as a 20-year-old spoiled oil heiress, I didn't give any thought to how I treated Marwell, and that was wrong of me in every way, shape, and form. And it was even more wrong to compare him to an ex-boyfriend from high school who now I haven't seen since high school. I was able to get Marwell that Rolex watch back then like it was nothing, but it was something big for him to buy me that hat box even though he couldn't afford to get me the crocodile version of it; most men couldn't. I found out later that he gave it to his mom to put her church hats in, and she said it was the best gift she'd ever received from anyone. I also found out that he married several years ago and now has two kids and is out of his sports profession but owns a successful business, and is able to give his wife and kids anything they want. I felt that if I acted right that I could be his wife, but as a result from my actions, I'm still single with no children while all of my siblings are happily married and have families except the youngest, Hollis, who is still childless . . . but she's married and I know she will probably have some great news to tell our family soon. I wanted to experience the joy of marriage and my own family, but didn't know if it would ever happen for me.

3
THE JOY OF PARTYING

My phone rang.

Hyacinth.

"Hy. What's going on?"

"What's going on with you? Hannah and Mom and Dad told me you're on your way here. I wanted you to leave early, Holly, since I know that you know by now why I wanted you to because of how bad it is out there."

"Yeah, I think I have some idea of how bad it is out here," I sarcastically replied, as I still could see barely ahead of me.

She sighed. "Come on, Holly. Don't act like such a brat, okay? We're just concerned about you getting here. It took Chris and me over an hour after the usual time we would usually get here since we have the baby and it was bad out, but now it's gone from bad to worse. Do you want me to stay on the phone with you?"

"No, I don't need another mom, okay? Like I said, I'll be fine. I have great music to listen to, my SUV is completely winterized, and I'm an excellent driver."

"Okay, but call us when you get close."

"I will."

"Oh, and another thing. I just wanna let you know that Avery is here."

"WHAT?!"

"See, I knew I was gonna get this reaction from you, Holly. Please keep calm, okay? We all want you to get here safe."

"Then you should not have told me about him being there."

"You were gonna find out he was here once you got here anyway, Holly. I just wanted to warn you."

"What the hell is he doing there?"

"Well, remember, he's the son of Dad's best friend. They've been best friends for decades."

"And I haven't spoken to Avery in almost a decade."

"And you don't have to speak to him when you get here, okay?"

"What made you think I was going to? Just what the hell is going on, Hy? Why is it that a flash from my past had to show up at an annual party that my parents throw? Oh, what? To throw it in my damn face about having things now that I don't?"

"Holly, I don't want you going off on him when you get here, okay? Especially since he didn't come here alone."

"Bye, Hy."

"Holly!"

Christmas Day, 9 Years Ago

"How the hell can you smoke that stuff? It smells like a skunk," I said, as Avery and I sat next to each other on a sofa passively watching a Christmas movie on mute in one of two guesthouses my parents had that were in the back of their house.

"I'm stressed, Holly, you know that," he said, and took another puff off of his weed.

"Well, you're lucky no one is staying in this house for the holidays this year otherwise there is no way we would be able to be in here."

"I know. But it's better to be in here than to be at that party. No offense, but it's too grown for me. It feels like a party for our parents, you know?"

"That's because it pretty much is. But they call it a friends and family party with close family and friends," I said, and took a sip of my holiday drink. "I'm so glad I'm 21 now that I can drink legally."

"That drink looks like it will pair awesome with this THC."

I laughed. "No thank you."

"Just try it. I don't wanna smoke alone, baby."

I held my breath as he held the joint to my mouth. I reluctantly opened my mouth and took an inhale . . . and exhaled into a frenzy of wild coughing!

He laughed and then took another drag. "Damn, baby! You never have smoked before, have you?"

"Just cigarettes—Nat Sherman—the colorful ones with the gold filter. But I don't smoke those all of the time. I gotta quit all of this stuff. I also like hookah—the kind that looks like lacquered colorful cigarettes that come in the pack with the different flavors and crystal tips? Eshish is my favorite, but I always gotta get them from the UK."

"Damn. Didn't know you lit up that much. You definitely don't have smoker skin or a cough, laugh, or whatever."

"Well, that's because I'm still young, but if I don't stop I will, and that can be sooner than I think. That 'Black don't crack' is a myth for a lot of us, and we've all seen proof. I'm not heavy with anything I smoke; nowhere near addicted."

"Speak for yourself," he said, and took another puff off of his weed. "This, baby, is what brings me joy."

"Are you serious?" I said with disgust. "We're not even supposed to be smoking it unless it's for medical reasons."

"My stress trying to complete my last year in college is my medical reason, doll."

"You're that pressured, huh?"

"Extremely," he said, and put the joint towards my mouth.

I leaned into it and took another puff off of it. "I can't go back to the house smelling like this. My dress reeks now."

"Yeah, so does my suit. And I don't wanna go back in there anyway. I know it's your parents' party, but like I said—no offense—it's pretty boring. My dad looks forward to it every year and so does my mom. But I think it's just a bunch of old people and bratty-ass little kids."

"Well, we're definitely in agreement with that!"

We laughed as we stared at each other as "Be Mine For Christmas" by Kem featuring Ledisi, played throughout the room.

"Love this song," he said as he smiled at me.

"Me too," I replied as I returned the smile.

People thought Avery and I would've been engaged to be married by now. My dad's best friend's son marrying one of his daughters was what people were waiting on. But I was waiting on him to ask me to be his girlfriend. But with the two of us only being 21, we felt as if our lives were just beginning. Our parents married around our age, so I guess it was only natural for them to think we would follow suit. But they had seen time and time again that times had definitely changed. But as the old saying goes, the more things change, the more they stay the same.

"So, what did you get for Christmas?" he asked, and then took another drag and blew the smoke in the air.

"We'll be here all night if I have to tell you everything."

He laughed. "Oh, I forgot, you're Holly Harper, of course. So, yeah, let me narrow it down. What gift did you get that you wanted the most? The one that brought you the most joy?"

"Well, since that disaster of a gift last Christmas from my for-a-year-now ex-boyfriend, I would have to say that getting my very first brand-new Hermes Birkin 25 in beautiful shiny red crocodile with palladium hardware from my parents brought me the greatest joy; totally instant. I unboxed it hours before everyone came to the party."

He looked less-than-impressed. "A handbag? *A handbag* gave you the greatest joy this Christmas?"

"It's a freakin' Birkin! A crocodile one! Of course! How many young women my age do you know have a Hermes Birkin bag of any size or color? And an authentic one and crocodile one at that?"

"Just you and your two older sisters. Am I right?"

"You're exactly right!" I proudly replied. "And Hollis can't wait until she's 21 because she pretty much knows by now that she's gonna be gifted one as well."

"And what was the big accomplishment you all have made to be able to be gifted one of the most expensive designer handbags made?"

"Do we have to accomplish anything? I mean, Hannah had graduated from college with a 4.0; Hyacinth had a 3.8 graduating from college as well. They're both also in our mom's sorority."

"And you?"

"College just wasn't for me. I wasn't gonna waste their money going."

"Understandable because it's not for everyone. Sometimes I don't think it's for me, but I have to go since I have to go straight to medical school after."

"Not if you don't want to."

"And not follow in my dad's footsteps? Are you kidding, Holly? Sorry I don't come from a billionaire oil family who were able to start several successful businesses with their generational wealth for decades."

"I can't help what family I was born into."

"None of us can. But we can help what we take and don't take for granted, especially on a day like today. And we can definitely create our own joy. But the best joy for ourselves is when we give joy to others."

"I know, Avery. I'm not selfish."

"Never said you were, Holly." He looked at his phone. "Rex just sent me a text. He wanted to know if I was gonna come to Diamante for their Christmas party tonight since he's working the door. It's going on right now and is supposed to last all night."

"Don't you have to be 25 to get in there?"

"You're Holly Harper, girl. Everyone knows who you are so you can get into anywhere."

"That's true! Okay, I'm definitely down. Let's leave now before it gets too crowded. Are you okay to drive us there?"

"Of course. I gotta smoke a lot more than this to feel some kind of high," he said, as he texted Rex back to tell him that we would be on our way.

Over 20 minutes later, Avery led me by hand as we made our way through the overcrowded Diamante club on this Christmas night as Run-DMC's "Christmas In Hollis" was played throughout it. From fancy holiday dresses and suits to ugly Christmas sweaters, this was the crowd we preferred to be in since everyone looked like they were around our age—even though you had to be four years older than us to legally get in—but we felt we fit right in.

"Hollis *swears* this song was made for her!" I laughed.

"Is that right?"

"Yeah, even though she wasn't even born when it first came out and neither was I!"

"Me neither!"

We laughed.

"You were right about us getting in here," I said as we made our way to a table his friend Rex had reserved for us.

"I told you it wasn't gonna be a problem," he said. "You see how they didn't even check our ID's—that even surprised me!"

"Me too! I think pulling up here in your dad's red Ferrari had a lot to do with it."

"That and you. They know who you are, Holly. Besides, Rex would've been able to get us in regardless. But I don't understand all of this crap about why you have to be 25 and older to get in here when there's only a 4-year age gap with 21 and 25. That has never made any sense to me."

"Me neither, but I'm glad to be who I am if it means being able to get into places where most my age couldn't."

"And using my dad's car to not have to wait in that long line out there, especially if Rex wasn't here!"

We laughed as we sat down at the table.

"So, is this party better than your parents' party?"

"Much better," I replied with a grin as I took in the atmosphere. "I guess I feel like I'm still too young for them even though I'm considered an adult now. I've grown up going to that party since they were having them before Hannah was even born. I just like to do what I wanna do now."

"And you're one of the very few out there who has the financial lifestyle to be able to do what you want so count your blessings in that aspect because not everyone is able. I guarantee you that you're the wealthiest person in this club."

"But I'm no different than anyone else."

"And that's what I like about you, Holly."

I nodded with a smile as New Edition's "All I Want for Christmas Is My Girl" played next.

He continued to smile at me. "Wanna dance?"

"Sure, why not?"

He held my hand as we walked out to the dance floor, and we danced to the song like everyone else, as I noticed the men singing the lyrics to their girl as it was clear they knew them by heart. Since I wasn't Avery's official girl, dancing to this song seemed a little too awkward.

"Do you miss having a man?" he asked as he smiled at me.

"Yes," I said, as I smiled up at him.

"Because I miss having a woman," he replied with a smile. He slowly leaned down to me as his lips were ready to touch mine.

I turned my head away.

He sighed. "Sorry."

"It's okay."

He sighed again as he stared over me as if he had made the biggest mistake of his life. I just didn't know how I felt about him kissing me, especially in a public place. He wasn't my boyfriend so he should not have been surprised that I politely refused his advances.

Song over.

We walked back over to the table, and if there was any time that I felt like I suddenly didn't know him anymore, it was right now. He seemed to have taken my rejection of him trying to kiss me very personally, but I didn't wanna give him the wrong idea since we were never seriously involved with each other since we were involved with other people all of the time, so this was the very first time the two of us were actually single. I didn't wanna ruin his Christmas by rejecting a kiss from him as if I was standing under the mistletoe, it's just that I was not feeling him on that type of level, so I didn't know why I was always wondering why he hadn't asked me to be his girlfriend yet. My signals were so mixed about him I honestly didn't know what and how to truly feel.

We didn't talk to each other for several minutes, so I was glad the music was good and there were a lot of people here that were having a great time.

"Excuse me," he said, as if we'd just met.

I nodded with a smile and took a sip of my drink as I still took in the atmosphere.

A half hour had passed.

No sign of Avery anywhere.

I got on my phone and called him.

No answer.

I texted him.

No answer.

I went to the front door to talk to his friend Rex. "Hey, Rex."

"Holly," he said with a smile. But it was something about me approaching him this time compared to how it was when Avery and I first got here.

"I haven't seen Avery in almost an hour. Do you know where he is?"

He sighed. "He left."

"LEFT?!"

He walked me over to an area less crowded. "Yeah, Holly. He left. And he didn't leave here alone."

"You're making this up," I said, as I tried to contain the little composure I had left since I was in public and it was Christmas.

"He told me the two of you got into a fight, so he said he was leaving."

"That's a lie. He was mad because I wouldn't let him kiss me while we were dancing! That asshole! Who did he leave with?"

"I don't know her. Some typical hoe. She's always up in here. I'm sorry, Holly."

I stormed off from him as I tried to suppress the tears that were welling up in my eyes. I couldn't believe he did this. He showed me exactly why I was never feeling him on that more-than-friends level. My signals about him were straightened out now. I went to an area of the club that was actually pretty quiet and got on my phone.

"Holly! Just where the hell are you?" Hyacinth said.

"Hy, please don't tell Mom and Dad."

"Holly, where are you? I'm not gonna ask you again."

"I need a ride home. Avery freakin' left me here."

"WHAT?!"

"I'm not kidding, Hy. I need a ride home. His friend just told me he left here with some club cunt."

"What happened? Why would he take you there then leave you there and take off with another woman and not tell you?"

"I don't wanna talk about it right now. I just wanna get out of here."

She let out a sigh. "For the last time—where are you, Holly?"

"Diamante."

"*Diamante?!* Are you serious? Why the hell did he take you to that ghetto-ass club for?"

"Because they are having a Christmas party and he could get us in because his friend works here; he's the one I just talked to."

"Yeah, I bet, because you have to be 25 to get in there. Okay, you owe me *big* for this one, Holly."

"I know. Please hurry."

4
THE JOY OF FAVORITES

"Thanks, Hy," I said, as I got into her Mercedes SUV.

"You're welcome," she said as she stared at me, and then pulled off down the street. "Never thought I would be coming here to pick you up at this type of club and on Christmas at that, Holly. You know better than that to come to a club like this—how the hell did he talk you into it?"

"Because the party at Mom and Dad's was boring as usual."

"Well, I'm not gonna a hundred percent disagree with that. But anything could've happened in Diamante despite it being Christmas."

"Yeah, you're right. But we were having a good time until I rejected him trying to kiss me."

"What?!" she said as she stared at me, and then focused her attention back on the road. "So that's what happened?"

"Yeah, it did. Some Christmas this has been. Two years in a row I've had my joy stolen from me. I'm sick of this happening, Hy, and this year it was not my fault."

"Well, it's clear how much Avery obviously likes you. If I can be very honest with you, I'm glad he's only been a friend to you because something has always seemed off about him."

I found what she said to be interesting. "What do you mean?"

"I actually can't point to anything specific, it's just that if y'all would've ever been serious about each other then I know you would've been doing it for our family and his."

"Yeah, *I* would've been!"

We laughed.

Tears welled up in my eyes.

"It's okay, Holly," she said, as she gave me a sympathetic pat on my shoulder. "Even though you're not attracted to him and actually showed it by rejecting his advances, it still hurt him a lot and it showed him how you really felt about him even though you didn't mean to hurt him. I also feel that even though he got his feelings hurt by you, he should not have left you all alone there in a place you'd never been to or didn't know anyone at, and I'm excluding his friend Rex since he's Avery's friend, not yours."

"And I think that's the thing I was the most pissed off about is what he did. It's like he didn't even care if something could've happened to me because anything could've. I mean, to leave and not tell me and not only leave, he left with some club chick who Rex told me is always up in there."

"Well, you're too good for that place. That chick probably won't see him after tonight. She's probably giving him all of the Christmas joy and jollies that he thought he was gonna get from you tonight."

"He wasn't gonna get a damn thing from me."

"And you showed him he wasn't. Good for you, Holly. But like I said, I don't like the fact that he left you there and in an area like that. That club is not in a good part of the city at all." She looked at my lap. "And you carried your Hermes Birkin there, too?"

"It was the only bag I had with me. Remember I just got it earlier today from Mom and Dad."

"Damn. I hope people didn't know how much a bag like that costs because you could've easily have been robbed. Very easily."

"I know, Hy. I just wanna forget about this Christmas, and I don't ever wanna see Avery again."

I looked at my Hermes Birkin bag as it sat on the passenger's seat of my car. I carried it every Christmas to their party since it was a Christmas gift from my parents. It was still just as beautiful now as it was when I got it nine years ago. I grinned as "Favorite Things" by Alicia Keys was now playing, and I absolutely loved the laid-back sexiness of this song. And I was unapologetic about my expensive handbags being some of my favorite things as well as a lot of things mentioned in this song, but I was still working on the drama-free thing like most, but knew that was true wishful thinking. I sighed as this snow was not letting up at all and was seemingly getting worse.

The snowplow was way ahead of me where I couldn't even see it or its flashing lights through the torrential snow and strong, relentless winds. Now I didn't care how long it was gonna take for me to get there since Hy informed me that Avery was there; like I really needed to know that. In fact, I didn't have to be there at all. I was still closer to home than I was there, and right now, I wasn't getting anywhere. I called Hy back.

"Holly! Hey! Are you almost here?"

"Not even close, Hy. Look, it's gotten worse and I don't even think I've made it even 2 miles. I think I'm just gonna turn around and head back home. I can barely see in front of me. I'll drop by later if this lets up."

"Okay, Holly. I'm sure Mom and Dad and everyone will understand. Chris and I barely got here ourselves with the baby. I'll let them all know."

"Okay, because I just don't think I need to be in the same house as Avery anyway so—"

I screamed as a semi-truck jackknifed in front of me!

"HOLLY!"

I swerved to avoid the truck and went spinning out of control as now everything looked like a blur in my vision, as everything in my past flashed before my eyes.

5
THE JOY OF SAVIOR

I thought I'd woke up from a nightmare—but I was still out here, but here in my SUV. It was still coming down hard as I realized that I'd spun off the road and into the parking lot of Joy's Soul Food Diner, a Black family-owned establishment that'd been here for decades. I looked around and noticed that my SUV was the only car in the parking lot. It was like a scene out of a movie where I had spun out and off the road and into a parking lot and ended up practically perfectly aligned in a parking spot right in front of the restaurant.

Unreal.

I tried to control my heavy breathing as I noticed no one came out here to see if I was okay. They were clearly open as it was indicated on a blinking neon OPEN sign right in the front of the restaurant. But the time indicated that it was still a little bit before it was officially Christmas, so people were at home celebrating with their family and friends so I understood why no one was here, but I thought at least *someone* would be here. But then again, who the hell would be crazy enough to get out in this weather unless like me, they were headed to a family or friends' home for a midnight Christmas party.

I continued to shake as I reached over to get my purse because I was gonna have to brave it and run in here because I just couldn't be in this SUV right now. I felt I was somewhat safe now and I didn't feel I was injured from the spinout. I looked to my left and screamed!

A man stood outside of my door!

I rolled down my window.

"Are you okay?" he asked, as he was completely covered up—ski mask and all.

"Yeah, I'm fine. I'm just shaken, that's all," I said, as the snow and ice whipped me in my face.

"Come on, I'll help you inside," he said.

"I'm not wearing any boots. I have on dressy sandals," I said.

"Seriously?"

"Yes, *seriously,*" I stressed, as I tried not to sound offended that he thought I was crazy to be wearing sandals during a blizzard, but what was crazier was that I didn't have any boots in here to put on just in case what'd happened had unfortunately happened.

"Okay," he said.

I opened my door and he immediately scooped me up out of my seat and carried me towards the door. Just in those few seconds, my feet felt like ice. He put me down right when we got in the door on a carpeted mat. "Thank you."

"You're welcome," he said, as I still couldn't see what he looked like. He looked down at my feet. "Wow, you weren't kidding. Those are some fancy holiday shoes. Can't blame you for not wanting to get snow and ice on them. Have a seat anywhere. The waitress will be with you in a minute."

"Thank you," I replied with a smile. I slowly walked on the black and white checkered floor and took a seat in one of the red leather booths as I checked out the Christmas decorations as Ella Fitzgerald's "Let It Snow! Let It Snow! Let It Snow!" played throughout the diner. I felt like I'd stepped back in time. It was nice and warm and inviting in here, and I hated to admit it, but I'd never been in here before. Passed it almost every day. My mom always said the Harper family "Don't do diners." I couldn't wait to show her where I unexpectedly ended up.

I looked up to an older man smiling at me as he sat on a stool at the end of the counter as he had a newspaper in one hand and a cigarette in the other. I guess this diner was still old-school in the sense that they still let people smoke in here. He nodded to me, I smiled back as I couldn't stop looking at him. He looked just like my Mark Roberts holiday drummer figurine—down to the gold circle wire-frame glasses he was wearing. His long white mustache that flowed into his even longer bright white beard made him perfect to play any holiday character, from Santa Claus to an elf. All he needed was a festive suit to put on.

I got on my phone as I almost forgot to call Hy back since the last thing I heard before I spun out was her screaming my name and the song on at the time fading into some sort of unexplained darkness as my past flashed in front of my eyes.

"HOLLY!" she screamed again.

"Hey, Hy. I'm all right."

"SHE'S OKAY!" she yelled out to everyone at the party.

"Holly! Holly! It's your MAMA!" Mom said, as it was obvious that she grabbed the phone from Hy.

"Hey, Mom. Merry Christmas. I'm all right, like Hy told you all."

"What happened, baby?"

"A semi-truck jackknifed in front of me, and in order for me to avoid running into it I swerved from it and spun out off the road and into the parking lot of Joy's Soul Food Diner."

"You serious, baby?"

"Yeah, I am, Mom. I swear I'm not making this up. A man who works here came out to see if I was okay and carried me inside since I'm wearing stilettos—open-toe ones."

"That was nice of him. Well, just stay there until the weather gets better. And let us know how the food is because I want you to get something to eat."

"I thought you didn't do diners," I reminded her. I looked at the old man as he looked at me. He cracked a grin and went back to reading his newspaper.

"I don't. I don't care where you ended up as long as you ended up in a safe place and you're off those roads."

"Yeah, I didn't get that far at all. I don't even think I got to barely two miles. It's still coming down bad out there," I said, as the cop cars and ambulances drove by to the obvious jackknifed truck with their flashing lights barely appearing through the storm. I started to realize just how lucky I was to be able to escape what could've been.

I picked up the menu and looked at it. Everything on it looked delicious. I almost saw instantly what I'd been missing for so many years. The best food wasn't always at the most expensive restaurants, but it was where my family had went more than half the time when we went out to eat, especially when I was younger. My mom didn't like us dining on fast food or at small diners and other restaurants that weren't up to her ridiculous standards. I thought it was very snooty of her to be that way, but very interesting now that she didn't care that I was here and it was all because of this blizzard.

What if there was no blizzard?

I had a million chances to come here when it wasn't like this, and I was only here because of how it was outside and I knew I would probably be here for a while and on Christmas day at that. I was starting to believe that this happened for a reason.

6
THE JOY OF REALIZATION

I watched as the Harper family social media manager livestreamed the party. I didn't see Avery anywhere, and I was gonna turn it off if I had. I really wasn't interested in who he was there with. The only thing I was interested in was his explanation as to why he did what he did to me nine years ago because he had yet to apologize to me for it. Anything could've happened to me that night, and if it had, I would've hoped that the guilt would've plagued him for the rest of his life.

"Hi, I'm Krista. I'll be your waitress for tonight," a young woman said as she stood with a coffee pot in her hand, along with a Santa Claus cap on her head, a short-sleeved tee that had the diner's logo on it in a red script, and blue jeans and sneakers. She looked tired and worn out, and I really felt sorry for anyone who had to work on this day as well as on Christmas because I felt that most had a right to be with their family.

"Hi, Krista. I'm Holly. Is that a fresh pot of coffee?" I had to ask as I always did at every restaurant I went to when I wanted some coffee, and I needed it bad right now.

"Yes, I just made it," she replied with a weary smile. She flipped over the mug on the table and moved it over to the pot.

"I don't drink out of anyone's coffee mugs but mine," I informed her. I pulled out my Prouna Christmas Delight Chain white mug with a shiny platinum handle and trim around the top and bottom, and adorned with beautiful green, red, and clear Swarovski Elements crystals in a four-row chain sparkling all around the bottom of the mug. I also pulled out the special coaster that came with it.

"What a beautiful mug," she said with a brighter smile.

"Thank you," I replied with an even bigger smile.

She filled my mug with the coffee.

"You can leave the pot here. I have a feeling I will be here for a while."

"No problem," she replied, and put a protector on the table and placed the pot on it. "Are you ready to order?"

"I'm still trying to decide," I let her know. I picked the menu back up and looked at it since I admitted to forgetting that I was here when the livestream of the party started. She nodded with a smile and walked away as I took a sip of my coffee as I watched her. I turned my attention back to the menu because I was getting hungry. I took another sip of my coffee and placed the mug down on the table as I stared at it.

Christmas Day, 7 Years Ago

"So, I know we opened our gifts at your house, but I forgot to give you this one," my boyfriend Caden said, and handed a beautifully wrapped box to me.

"Thank you," I replied with a smile, as I sat in my old bedroom at my parents' house during their party. It pretty much still looked the same as it had when I left it when I turned 18, and I always came in here on Christmas during the party with my boyfriend. And this was our second year in a row in here, so I felt really good about the direction our relationship was going. I was hoping what I was about to open was gonna be the start of our official future together, but the box was way too big to be an engagement ring, but maybe he was trying to fool me into thinking that it wasn't.

I ripped the wrapping off of it to a black box:

PROUNA JEWELRY.

I flashed him a confused but curious look. I opened the box . . . to a beautiful white mug with four rows of sparkling red, green, and clear crystals circling the mug towards the bottom. I smiled as I looked at it as the crystals just danced in the lights in this room.

"Now you can drink your coffee in style during the holiday season," he said with a smile.

"I always drink my coffee in style. I have several of these mugs in different colors and styles, but you knew which one to get me because I don't have the Christmas one. Thank you."

"You're welcome, baby."

We kissed.

"And thank goodness that you don't. I even made sure by looking in the cabinets in your kitchen to make sure."

"Well, at least you did that," I said with a smile as I still looked at it. "I can't believe you bought me a coffee mug that costs $189—and that's not for a six-or-10 pack of them."

"Well, I could afford it, because nothing's too much for my baby!" He kissed me again as I smiled. He gave me a concerning look. "Something wrong?"

I put the mug on my bed as I got up.

"Holly? What is it?" he asked, as he still sat on the bed. "Do you really like the mug?"

"Yeah, I think it's beautiful and it pretty much completes my collection of them since I don't know when they're gonna come out with any new ones. I just thought—"

He gave me a concerned look. "What? What did you think?"

I shrugged as I looked out the window at the light snowfall.

He got up off of my bed and came over to me. "Holly?"

I looked at him.

"Talk to me."

I mustered up a smile. "It's nothing, okay? Let's get back down to the party. I'm gonna have one of the waitresses put on my mom's Christmas specialty coffee and I'm gonna pour it right in this mug."

"That's my girl!" he said with a big smile. "I gotta use the bathroom. Excuse me."

I nodded with a smile as he walked into the bathroom attached to my room. And being in this room brought back so many Christmas memories. Before the boys, before the everything. I thought he wanted to come in here because he was going to propose to me right here in my childhood room at this party on Christmas Day. Now I had all of my joy once again on this day wiped away. I sighed and wondered if I was ever gonna have a joyful Christmas again.

I looked at his coat as it sat on the sofa. I looked towards the bathroom as he was still in there. I quickly searched through every pocket of it . . . .

And came across a black box.

And it was small in size. I opened it up . . . .

To a 7-carat marquis diamond solitaire engagement ring!

I almost shrieked in excitement as I tried not to let the tears well up in my eyes since I was wearing full makeup. I couldn't believe it!

He was gonna propose to me after all!

Something told me to look inside his coat to see if there was another small box hiding in it, and I was right!

I looked inside the ring . . . .

To Elizabeth . . . The Love of My Life

If there was any time I felt like I was gonna lose it for good then this was the time.

Caden emerged from the bathroom. "Hey." He looked down at my left ring finger as I sarcastically wore the ring he was giving to someone else. He gasped and then sighed. "Holly . . . ."

"So I get the Christmas mug and Elizabeth is getting the 7-carat diamond engagement ring," I said as calmly as I could, as I looked down at it still on my finger, and then glared back up at him.

"Holly . . . I was gonna tell you when the time was right, *I swear* I was. She's pregnant—"

"GET THE FUCK OUT OF MY PARENTS' HOUSE!" I yelled! I took off the engagement ring and threw it at him! "GET OUT!"

He picked up the ring and ran past me as he quickly grabbed his coat as I quickly grabbed the Christmas mug he'd just given to me as a gift. I chased him out of the room as everyone came to a standstill as he ran down the hall and down the right side of the black wrought-iron double staircase as I still ran after him with the mug in my hand.

"What is going on?!" Mom asked, as now almost everyone at the party was in the foyer.

"AND TAKE YOUR MUG WITH YOU! I HATE YOU!" I screamed, and threw it at him as he ran past the security men for this party, but it missed him and hit the wall and smashed into pieces!

Everyone gasped as I collapsed on the staircase and burst into tears as my family tried their best to comfort me and get the whole story from me.

As it turned out, Caden was seeing both of us at the same time. Him and Elizabeth were high-school sweethearts. They'd never completely stopped seeing each other even though they took breaks from each other here and there, and I'd found out that we'd met during one of his here-and-there breaks with her. I'd also found out that he was gonna propose to her the next day . . . and he did . . . and she accepted, despite what went down between the two of us the day before. I felt used by him to say the least, and friends of mine confirmed to me that he wanted to be with me more for the fact that I was Holly Harper, the billionaire oil heiress, than me being just plain-old Holly who wanted a serious, unconditional loving relationship. But in the end, Elizabeth won him by way of a pregnancy, and got all of the joy starting with that engagement ring; all of that joy that I thought was supposed to be for me and only me. And she was still having all of the joy to this day.

7
THE JOY OF COMFORT

I continued to stare at my Prouna Christmas Delight coffee mug, the same style I threw back at Caden seven years ago. I loved the mug so much that I felt enough time had passed and since it was still being sold, I decided to get another one—but it cost me $210 this time around. I don't know why I was carrying it with me to the party since I didn't mind drinking out of the mugs at my parents' home, I guess I just needed something to talk about while I was there, and the fact that I destroyed the one he gave me but was able to buy as many as I wanted for myself.

I looked up and saw my food headed my way, and it smelled delicious, and that was a word I didn't throw around all of the time. I moved everything out of the way because I ordered a lot because I'd never had their food before, plus, it was Christmas . . . officially.

"Here you, go, Holly. Merry Christmas. Enjoy," Krista said with a smile.

"Wow, everything looks great. Thank you, Krista. Merry Christmas to you, too."

"Thank you," she replied with a surprised smile as if I wasn't gonna wish her the same, and maybe that was the impression she got of me.

I ate my three fried piece combo of fried chicken, fried pork chops, and fried fish like no one was watching. I dove into these collard greens in between, and practically inhaled the mac and cheese. I couldn't even remember the last time I had soul food, but I never remembered it being this good when I had. This was comfort food at its finest. I had to slow myself down since I was eating so fast, so I took a few sips of my lightly sweetened iced tea.

I turned it back on the private livestream of the party since I knew it had officially started now since it was officially Christmas.

"MERRY CHRISTMAS, HOLLY!" my family said as they waved to me with their children and all.

"Merry Christmas, everyone," I replied with a smile.

"We see you're eating. How's the food?" Dad asked.

"Wonderful," I replied with a smile. "I see now what I've been missing since this is the first time I've been here." I looked at Mom as she smiled with a nod.

"Are you the only one in there?" Hannah asked.

"No. There's an older gentleman here sitting at the end of the counter reading a newspaper," I replied.

"A physical copy of the newspaper?" my brother Howard asked with a grin.

Everyone laughed.

I looked up at the older man as he still tended to his newspaper as if no one else was around. "Yeah, it's a physical copy of one."

"I didn't think people read physical copies of newspapers anymore," Hollis said. "I've never seen one in person."

"Yeah, and you just gave away your age saying that," I said.

Once again, we all laughed.

"Um, I wanna get back to eating so you all have fun and I'll try to get there as soon as I can."

"Take your time, baby. But you know there's plenty of food here for you as well."

"I know, Mom, but I'll just eat it later on today."

"Okay, baby."

I disconnected the call and continued eating.

Krista came back over to me. "How is everything?"

"Wonderful, just like I told my family."

"So that's who you were talking to?"

"Yes. I'm supposed to be at my parent's annual Christmas party, but for the first time ever, I'm missing it because of this weather. Had I known it was gonna be like this then I would've stayed at their house overnight last night, or at least got there earlier yesterday before the storm."

"Yeah, I definitely understand. This storm seemed to have come out of nowhere. Luckily I've been here since yesterday afternoon."

"Yesterday afternoon? Wow, Krista. That's a long time to be here."

"Well, no one was gonna work a double, plus, I didn't have any family and friends to celebrate this Christmas with for this year."

"I'm sorry," I said as I lowered my head.

"It's okay. I know I'm gonna have to get used to it."

I wanted to ask her why would she have to get used to not being with family during what was supposed to be the most joyous time of the year, but I didn't wanna seem nosey, so I changed the subject. "Um, who cooked my food?"

"Rudy," she replied with a smile.

"Rudy? Was he the one who came outside to see if I was okay after I spun into this parking lot and carried me in here?"

"He sure was. He saw your spinout on the security monitor. I'm sorry I didn't rush out there with him. He wanted me to stay in here in case we got any calls or whatever—from who and for what, I don't know. I knew no one was gonna get out in this mess."

"Yeah, and I only got out in it because I live only five miles from my parents' house, but tonight it seemed like fifty miles, and as you see, I didn't make it."

"It would've been hard for anyone to make it anywhere no matter how close their destination is."

"You're right, Krista," I said with a smile. But I admit to being curious about Rudy. "Um, is Rudy busy? I just wanna thank him again for coming out to my car and carrying me in here. Plus, I wanna personally tell him how good this food is."

She smiled. “No, he’s not busy—at least I don’t think he is—I’ll go get him. Can I get you anything else while I’m back there?”

“Not yet, but I would like some dessert later on.”

“You got it,” she replied with a smile. “Oh, by the way, your outfit is beautiful. Those Dolce&Gabbana pants are even more beautiful in person. And I would’ve had a man carry me in here too if I had on those Rene Caovilla shoes.”

I gasped as I was completely stunned that she knew exactly who my pants and shoes were by. I guess I had some very deep misconceptions about how only a certain class of people knew all about certain brands, and I saw just how ignorant I really was. “Thank you, Krista.”

“You’re welcome,” she said, and walked away from the table.

I looked at the older man who was still sat at the end of the counter reading his newspaper and still smoking like a chimney. He smiled at me as Krista walked by him and nodded to me once again. I smiled in return, all the while still thinking about her knowing about what I was wearing. I didn’t know why I couldn’t stop thinking about it. I felt so judgmental by being so surprised about a waitress in a diner knowing exactly who my pants and shoes were by, but it was definitely something about her knowing about my outfit—I know I wasn’t thinking too much into this or at least I’d hoped I wasn’t—I just didn’t know what it was.

8
THE JOY OF CONVERSATION

"Yeah, I'm still eating. The food is so good here I have the right mind to order everything else on this menu. I don't even know if I'm gonna be hungry for the party food later on," I said, as I still ate my early morning Christmas meal.

"We still have plenty of food here for you, baby. You know you don't have to worry about that," Mom said.

"And I have to thank a man by the name of Rudy who cooked all of this food for me. He's—"

"You're welcome."

I looked up to a very handsome man standing at my table smiling down at me. He had on the same type of uniform Krista had on, but he was wearing a red apron. "Mom, I'm gonna have to call you back." I hung up while I stared up at him with a big smile on my face.

"I'm Rudolph Joy the Third. I go by Rudy for short."

"Nice to meet you, Rudy. I'm Holly Harper," I said with a smile.

"Nice to meet you, Holly," he replied with a smile.

We shook hands.

"Please, have a seat if you wish," I said, and wiped my mouth.

"Thank you," he said, and sat right across from me. "It's nice to meet you, Holly Harper. Never thought I would actually meet one of the Black billionaire heiresses."

"You know who I am?" I asked, shocked that he actually knew.

"Who doesn't?" he said with a bright smile that exposed his perfectly straight white teeth.

"You said your last name is *Joy*? You have some relation to the people who own this restaurant?"

"I own the restaurant along with my dad. My grandfather is the one who opened it with my grandmother in 1947. It's always been in our family. It's in all of our wills to never sell it. It's the only business we got."

"That's great, Rudy. It's important for everyone who builds something to keep what is theirs. And I see why you've been in business for as long as you have because this food is absolutely delicious."

"Thank you. Secret recipes are the key to great food. Is this your first time here?" he asked with a curious grin.

"Yes," I replied with the head hang of shame. I slowly lift my head along with my eyes to find him still smiling at me.

"I'm glad you didn't get hurt out there," he said, as he looked out the window as it was still coming down hard, but not as much as it was when I spun out into this parking lot.

"Yeah, I'm glad I didn't, either. I'd never been so scared before in my life when that happened."

"Where were you headed out in weather like this?"

"To my parents' Christmas party. They have it every year and expected everyone to always be there before midnight. I didn't know there was a storm of this magnitude on the way and it completely caught me off guard when the garage door opened. Since my parents live only five miles away, I thought I could still make it, but as you saw, it just got worse and worse out there."

"Yeah, it did. I've been here for almost two days straight since everyone else had the day off today and yesterday. We're open 24/7 and have been since we've been in business. It's just me and Krista working, so if what didn't happen to you didn't happen, we would still be waiting on someone to come in here and get some of this food."

"Well, I think things happen for a reason," I said with a smile. "I'm glad that since I spun out of control into a parking lot and got stuck that it was here; don't know how I would feel anywhere else."

He nodded with a sexy smile. "I'm glad you feel that way about being here."

"I honestly do. And thank you again for carrying me in here. I honestly didn't know how I was gonna get in here with these shoes on. My feet have been nice and warm for hours now. I usually would wear boots, but my parents have a ten-car garage and I was just gonna pull my SUV into it and walk straight into their house without ever having to step outside."

"That explains why you're wearing those shoes. I'm glad I was of some help."

"I'm glad you were, too."

We continued to stare at each other as I sipped my coffee.

"That's a fancy mug. No wonder why you didn't wanna drink out of mine."

"Sorry," I said with true embarrassment. "I act like this at every restaurant."

"I'm not taking it personal," he replied with a smile. "At least you're being honest."

"Yeah, I feel it's the only way to be, even though the asshole who gave me the first one like this wasn't. I just liked it so much it took me years to buy another one. Sorry for swearing, especially on Christmas."

He chuckled in surprise at my profanity. "It's okay."

I looked down at his left ring finger and noticed he wasn't wearing a wedding ring. But usually someone like him did have someone special in their lives so I would not have been surprised at all if he had. And there was no way I was gonna ask. I didn't need any disappointing news on Christmas like all of the ones in the past.

"So, tell me about Holly Harper. I know she has to be a lot different from what I see on social media."

Not really, I thought. But here was my chance to have an honest conversation with someone I just met, someone who came out of this restaurant to see if I was okay and carried me in here. Someone who cooked my food and he can cook which is something that is always a plus to me.

"Well, I hate to say that I'm not that different from what you have seen of me on social media. But that's the part of me I feel that has to change. The same things keep happening to me year after year because I haven't made an effort to change them. I love being Holly Harper, the Black billionaire heiress, but that's all people see me as. Since I'm 30 years old now, I just wanna try and reinvent myself, but it's kind of hard to do that when I live a life that most people dream of. I feel like I've been everywhere in this world and have done everything—but I know there's so much more out there than exotic vacations and fancy clothes and everything."

He grinned as he looked down at my pants. "You definitely have fancy style. Krista was raving about your outfit back there in the kitchen. She didn't think she would ever see a woman in here with that type of look on, much less *the* Holly Harper."

"And I'm sorry I haven't been here a lot more. I feel like I just miss out on so many wonderful things because of the life I live. Things that I would never experience. Sometimes I feel like I have nothing real to look forward to."

"Why do you say that?"

I shrugged. I really didn't wanna get into this with him, but I did tell him to sit down so what did I really expect? Besides, we were the only ones in here besides Krista and the older gentlemen who obviously had no interest in holding a conversation with me, but he probably thought that more about me not wanting to hold a conversation with him than I thought that about him. Besides, I was always told that people his age just wanna be left alone. "Well, I'm the only one in my family who isn't married now; and I don't even wanna get into all of the bad relationships I've been in."

He smiled. "We all have. Unfortunately, I've seen some of the ones you've been in on social media like most."

"And that's just it. I'm tired of having my business all out there for everyone to talk about. Sometimes I just wanna be an ordinary girl. Now I know what I wanted to wish for at my parents' Midnight

Christmas Wishes party—to be a normal, ordinary girl. To have the joy my parents and my siblings have of being in a real, meaningful relationship. I pretty much wish this on every Christmas, but it's the one thing I don't get. I've been so hurt on Christmases in the past that this time of the year has almost become a former favorite time of the year."

"I'm sorry to hear that. That sounds rough. This is a day people should be joyful on, but it's hard when you don't have that special person to share it with. It's like you're always thinking you've done something wrong."

"I do," I replied, and took another sip of my iced tea. "Can I have some more tea?'

"Absolutely," he replied with a smile. He got out his phone and pressed a button.

No more than a few minutes later, Krista walked towards us with a pitcher of tea. She poured some in my glass. "Do you want me to leave it here?" she asked me.

I looked at Rudy as he grinned at me because I'm sure she told him about me wanting her to leave the coffee pot here earlier. "No, I'm good."

She nodded with a smile and left.

"So, how come you're not with your family?" I asked, assuming that he had one even though he wasn't wearing a wedding ring.

"I'm single. Single with no children," he informed me with a smile. "My last girlfriend actually broke up with me on Christmas two years ago to be with a man she thought would give her a better life."

"Wow," I said, as I shook my head. "And you own this nice diner. Like my family, you have something built in your family that has lasted for decades. People seem like they're always wanting better."

"And there's nothing wrong with that, but there is something wrong when a person acts like they don't wanna help someone build on what they have, and she wasn't willing to help me out. She wanted someone like your brother from a billionaire family."

"My brother is married; married to a woman he's been with since high school. They were pretty much the only Black couple at the school. He was told to stay away from certain women just like my sisters and I were told to stay away from certain men, especially when we left high school."

"I was told the same thing. And I'm lucky it didn't work out with her because she's got two kids by two different men since breaking up with me, and no, neither one of those men have anything to their names. So much for wanting someone who could provide her a better lifestyle."

I laughed. "Yeah, that's what she gets. Well, her loss is definitely someone else's gain."

"It sure is," he replied with a smile.

"So, where are your parents?"

"They're at their vacation home in Jamaica. They go there every other Christmas. They leave it up to me and my staff to run everything here."

"Well, they can relax in knowing that you all do an excellent job since it's only the two of you here. I'm already putting in a great recommendation."

He nodded with a smile. "And I appreciate that, Holly. We all do."

The chiming of the bells sounded, and it was the first time I'd heard them since Rudy carried me in here. He looked up since he was facing the front door. Someone else had just walked in here.

9
THE JOY OF LOYALTY

"Sterling! You made it, man!" Rudy said as he got up out of his seat.

I looked back to see a man who was just as bundled up as Rudy was when he came out of here to help me out of my SUV. He obviously knew exactly who he was, and he'd looked like a real-life snowman as he stood in front of Rudy as he began to unwrap himself out of his winter gear.

"Sorry it took me so long, man," Sterling said as he took off his coat and hung it up on a coat rack. "That was the most brutal storm I ever had to walk through to get here. Glad you gave me enough time to do so."

"I'm sorry you had to get out in it, man. I thought there would be more people here by now, but when Krista and I saw how bad it was getting, we realized that no one was gonna get out in this, except for one."

I looked back once again. They stared at me with a smile. I got up and walked over to them.

"Holly Harper! Right here in Joy's Soul Food Diner! Am I dreaming?" Sterling said with a big smile.

I blushed. "It's me. I'm Holly Harper."

"Holly, this is Sterling Goode, he works here. One of best employees ever," Rudy said with a smile.

"Nice to meet you, Sterling," I said, and held my hand out.

We shook hands, and his hand was ice cold even though I saw him with gloves on.

"It's an honor to meet you, Holly, especially on Christmas and in weather like this. What brought you out in it?" Sterling asked.

"My parents' Christmas party. I only live five miles from their house; got to barely two miles before I spun out trying to avoid a semi that jackknifed right in front of me right into this parking lot."

"For real? It sounds like a movie!" Sterling said.

"It's on our surveillance video," Rudy informed him.

"Wow, I bet that will get millions of views especially because of who you are," Sterling said. "But I'm glad you're okay. I knew when I saw that SUV out there, I knew it was a rich person in here that probably got stuck here, but to spin out and end up in here is something else entirely."

"Yeah, I felt like I was in a movie for a second. Rudy was definitely my savior for tonight. I was caught off-guard with the storm as well but thought I could make it."

"Well, you tried!" Sterling said. "Glad we were here for you."

I looked at Rudy as he smiled back at me. "Me too." I looked at the older gentleman as he nodded at me with a smile. I thought by now he'd read every article and ad in that newspaper.

"I'm gonna go back out there in about a half hour and take care of that parking lot since the storm seems to be letting up a little," Sterling said to Rudy.

"Okay, man. I appreciate it. Krista is in the back so she can hook you up with something."

"Good, because walking all of those miles for hours got me hungry!" Sterling said with a laugh. "Nice to meet you again, Holly."

"Nice meeting you, too," I replied with a smile.

Rudy and I sat back down at my table.

"He *walked* here? In this weather?"

"Yeah, he walks every day. Never makes any excuses about why he can't get here. I told him to stay home when I found out that the storm was coming, but his wife told me he'd already left. I tried calling him, but kept getting his voicemail, and I wanted to speak directly to him."

"How far does he live from here?"

"Seven miles southwest of here," Rudy said.

"Wow. Just wow," I said. I was so speechless I couldn't say anything else. This man had to walk farther than I had to drive. "No one should be out in this weather. No one. Much less walking in it."

"I know, Holly. But some people have no choice. Like I said, that alone makes Sterling the best employee I've ever had; my dad said so as well. He's employee loyalty at its finest."

"And I believe that," I replied with a smile. I looked outside to see if Rudy was actually telling me the truth about Sterling walking here in this blizzard. I didn't see any other cars in the parking lot except mine, and I could barely see it. I saw firsthand what people had to do just to get to work every day—and it went beyond loyalty. It was very eye-opening and made me take a good look at myself and the life I lived.

A half hour later, the blizzard diminished to flurries, and I was hoping it would stay this way. I was really enjoying myself in here, and especially my conversation with Rudy, and was hoping we could become friends. I looked outside and saw Sterling hard at work plowing the parking lot so people could get in here, not spin out in here like what I did. He really had his work cut out for him.

Krista walked towards me with another pot of fresh coffee. She placed it on the table. "Freshly made," she confirmed.

"Thank you," I replied with a smile.

She looked at my coat. "Is that beautiful coat Giorgio Armani?"

"Yes!" I said with surprise that I couldn't even hide. "You have great taste. You noticed my shoes and pants and everything."

"There's a reason," she said with a smile.

Now she had my interest totally piqued.

"What's the reason?" I asked.

She sighed. "I used to able to afford clothes and shoes like that."

"You're kidding!" I blurted out in shock. "Oh, my goodness. Sorry.

I'm so sorry I said that. That totally came out wrong and was completely inappropriate."

She smiled. "It's okay, Holly. Most wouldn't think a waitress working in a diner lived a life of glamour and jet-set glitz, but I did. And it was not that long ago. But I never thought in a million years I would be working as a waitress in a diner and especially on Christmas at that. It's amazing how someone's life can change for the better and then for the worse. But this is my reality and it looks as if it's gonna be this way for a while."

"I'm so sorry, Krista. On my way to my parents' party and in here, I was sulking and reminiscing on bad Christmases I had in the past because of relationships with men that ended in all different ways—some were due to me, some weren't. I just wish now that I could've been with my family, but now I hear that you lived a great life. I knew there was something much more to you knowing about what I was wearing and carrying."

She nodded with a smile. "Once a premier designer diva, always one, even though it's vicariously for me once again. I just don't know if things are ever gonna be the same with my husband and family and everything. But I'm loyal to him, I'm loyal to Rudy and the Joy family because they were the only ones who hired me after my husband went to prison."

"Prison? My goodness. What happened?"

"He's in a federal prison. The case is so complicated, but I believe him when he tells me he's innocent. He's been in there for two years now. I hate taking my kids there because it's just no place to take kids to."

"What's your husband's name?"

"Marwell Garland."

10

THE JOY OF COMPASSION

"Holly, I'm so sorry. I had no idea he was your ex-boyfriend from ten years ago. He never told me, *I swear* he didn't," Krista said, and quickly ate some more of her banana pudding.

I invited her to have dessert and coffee with me since I'd found out she was the one who was married to Marwell. I guess so many years had gone by that I really did forget about him and just didn't wanna know who he married and started a family with and who he built a great successful life with—but then Krista told me this, and on Christmas at that. She had my undivided attention as I tried not to eat the delicious peach cobbler in record time because it was the best I'd ever had.

"And I believe you, Krista. My relationship with Marwell didn't end on a good note at all. Now I know why I was thinking about him when I tried to get to my parents' party earlier. Never in a million years did I ever think I was gonna meet his wife in a restaurant."

"And me waiting on you at that. Can't make this up, huh?" she asked with a smile, and took a sip of her coffee.

"You absolutely can't," I replied with a smile. "I really blew it with Marwell. I honestly didn't deserve him back then. I was young—really young—and thought the whole world owed me everything even when I was getting everything because of my lifestyle. But what I wasn't getting was a deep, loving and meaningful relationship, and out of all of the boyfriends and almost-boyfriends I had, I believe Marwell was the most honest, and especially honest with me the night he broke up with me. I'm glad he found you. Like I said, I didn't deserve him and I will always stand by that."

"Wow, Holly. It's like I can't believe I'm hearing you say all of this. I would think he would've at least told me you're an ex-girlfriend of his since everyone pretty much knows who you are."

I cracked a grin. "He obviously wanted to forget about me that much, and I can't say I blame him. But what happened with the two of you? I'd heard how he was married and had a successful business going, but now I meet you and you tell me he's in prison. I thought you were joking."

"I wish I was." She shook her head and took another sip of her coffee. "He used to be a professional athlete, but of course you already know that."

"I do. That was his profession when we were together."

"But he only played less than three years. He opened his financial advisor business after getting advice from his agent to do so because even his agent said he was good at saving money and investing it and everything, so he had enough money to open his business with by the time he was officially done playing professional sports."

"When did you meet him?"

"Nine years ago at a Christmas party on Christmas. I was a waitress at the now-defunct club Lassier, and just to think I wasn't supposed to work that day. I was filling in for a girl who was on vacation."

"Wow, that was almost exactly one year later after he broke up with me. And to think I was at my parents' Christmas party when the two of you met. Unbelievable."

"Yeah, it is. Now that I think about it it's really amazing that he could've still been with you at the time."

"He took all what he was gonna take of me. But I will always appreciate how honest he was with me about why he ended things with me. Like he said, I was an entitled monster and he just couldn't afford to keep up with my need for material things. He told me he was nowhere near the highest-paid athlete and that he had to save his money to get me what he got me for Christmas."

"What was it?"

"A Louis Vuitton hat box."

"I know exactly what it is. I had one but had to sell it for money when Marwell went to prison. I also had a Hermes Birkin 25—a denim blue one—had to sell that, too. Yours is absolutely gorgeous. Truly a dream bag."

"Thank you, Krista. But I already had all of the sizes for the hat box it in the monogram print, and thought he was gonna get me a crocodile one; the orange one."

"Wow. That's a dream hat box for me. Especially now. But I had to sell a ton of things in the years since he's been in prison. I have really none of those nice things left, but it's all material things. I still have my kids, and my parents try and help out as much as they can, but they don't have much, and I don't wanna take away the little they have."

"I'm so sorry to hear all of this, Krista. You are such a wonderful person. I knew that when you first came to my table. I see why Marwell married you and broke up with me and never looked back."

"Thank you, Holly. It's been very hard not having him here for the past couple of holiday seasons, but I'm hanging in there. Gotta stay strong for my kids."

"Where are your kids?"

"They're in a back room sleeping. They've been sleeping since you got here. Ran themselves tired right before you got here. They knew it was Christmas Eve and they were excited like always. They're still too young to realize what's going on since they're only 4 and 6 years old. I didn't have anywhere else to take them this year."

"Again, I'm so sorry, Krista. No one should spend any holidays without their loved ones. I'm here because of sheer happenstance since I was on my way to be with my family like I've done every Christmas since moving out of their house. But, if you don't mind, could you tell me how Marwell ended up in prison? It just seemed like ten years went by so fast and now I'm hearing all of this about him?"

"No problem at all, Holly. To make a long story short, he's currently serving a 10-plus-year sentence for investment fraud. I think he was set up by his partner, someone who was with him from the start and helped him start his business. His partner convinced him to get into short-term promissory notes, and people were scammed out of millions of dollars. His partner was the one who handled most of the accounts, and Marwell trusted him. We seem like we lost everything overnight. We have nothing now. Once he's out of prison, we have to start all over."

"Wow, I can't believe I'm hearing this, Krista. Marwell always seemed so honest and was never in any trouble. You all just have to keep fighting in this case. I believe he is innocent like he told you he is. It's unfortunate that people get caught up in illegal business dealings all the time with partners who tell them to trust them and that they know what they're doing."

"Exactly, Holly. I believe his partner started this business with him so he could scam people, but Marwell let him handle everything, but he's one of the owners so he went down for it, too."

"I hope Marwell has a good lawyer or lawyers."

"I feel he does. I just spoke to him hours before you got here."

"Before I spun into here, huh?" I asked with a grin.

She laughed. "Yes, before you spun into here! And he said he's still fighting his case and won't stop until the truth comes out about the fact he had nothing to do with it."

"I don't even have to know all of the facts in the case to know that he had nothing to do with what you're telling me, Krista. Marwell has always been a very compassionate, loyal, honest person. He didn't realize it at the time and I actually didn't myself, but he taught me a lot about myself, and I thought about that a lot throughout the years. I knew I had to change a lot about myself for the better, and I feel I have, but there's a lot I'm still working on; I'm definitely a work in progress. If there was any boyfriend I thought could've been my husband back then, it was him. But he had all he was gonna take from me, and he broke up with me just hours before my favorite holiday and I one hundred percent deserved it. I'm glad he has someone like you."

"Thank you, Holly," she said with a smile.

Suddenly, a bunch of cars and SUVs came dashing into the parking lot.

Sterling burst through the doors seconds later. "We better call the rest of our staff and tell them to get here! We got some very wealthy customers!"

I looked out the window and did a double take. "That's MY FAMILY!"

11
THE JOY OF GOOD(E)

"MOM! DAD! What are you all doing here?!" I asked in complete shock and surprise as they all came through the doors with the Christmas party in tow. Everyone was still dressed in their fancy Christmas party clothes and some of the children were Christmastime wide-eyed, as I called it, while some were already Christmas crashed in their parent's arms with their mouths wide open.

"Everyone had a taste for some Christmas soul food!" Mom said with a smile as she took off her coat and put it on one of the booths in the diner.

"And since the roads are much better, we decided to bring the Christmas party to you, baby," Dad said with a smile. "Wow! It smells *good* in here!"

"What did you all do with the food at the party?" I asked.

"We had a local homeless shelter come pick it up," Mom said with a smile.

"Fabulous," I said with a smile.

Rudy walked out from the back as everyone took their seats and just from them being here, the diner was completely filled up with people sitting in the booths to being at the counter. I never thought I would see it this filled this fast, and it was with all of my family and friends.

I grabbed on to his hand. "Everyone, this is Rudy Joy. He's the owner of this diner."

"Hello, Harper Family. Nice to meet you all. It's an honor," Rudy said, and my family introduced themselves to him one by one.

"And it's an honor to meet the man of the family whose diner has been here for decades," Dad said with a smile.

"Thank you, Mr. Harper," Rudy said with a smile. "I have a lot of staff on their way here, but we can get you all hooked up with some of our Christmas drinks and specialties."

"We look forward to it," Mom said with a big smile, as she noticed that I was still holding Rudy's hand.

I slowly let go of his hand; he looked at me and smiled. "Um . . . *I swear* I didn't call them to tell them to come here," I told him.

"I believe you. But this is quite a surprise, and an unexpected Christmas gift for me and for this diner since I never thought I would ever have even one of the members of the Harper family come in here, much less the whole family and guests from your family's party."

"Well, it was clear I sold them on how good the food is here. And I just wanna say that I'm sorry again that it took us so long to come here."

"No apology necessary, Holly. The fact of the matter is, you're here now and not only are you here, your entire family is here with your other family and friends. This is great for business. I'm gonna have to get video and pictures of this and send it to my parents in Jamaica. Do you mind?"

"Mind? Absolutely we don't mind! We'll pose for you!" I said with a laugh.

He laughed as well. "Okay, I'll try and get some before you all leave. I wanna get started on these drinks and specialties. Krista is probably back there arguing to herself about me not helping her yet."

"Okay, I'll let you go," I said with a laugh.

I walked around the diner as it looked like the Midnight Christmas Wishes party was held here instead of at my parents' home as Herbie

Hancock's "Deck the Halls" played throughout the diner, and the older gentleman still sat at the end of counter doing his thing. I guess he wasn't giving up his seat for anyone.

"HOLLY!" Hannah yelled to me.

I walked over to her as she, Hyacinth, and Hollis sat in a booth together. Howard and their husbands sat in another booth. And every booth was filled in here and it didn't even look like this an hour ago. I smiled with pride since they genuinely surprised me with doing this. I sat down in the booth next to Hollis.

"So, what was up with you holding Rudy's hand?" Hannah asked with a curious grin that I knew all too well.

Hyacinth and Hollis looked at me the same way.

"What was wrong with me holding his hand? He went out there in that blizzard to see if I was okay. He carried me in here when I told him I was wearing these shoes, and he's been such a nice host. Someone was really here when I needed someone the most, and that someone is him. He even sat with me while I ate; I insisted that he did."

"Very nice of him. So you're getting to know him?" Hollis asked.

"Not really," I said with my head down.

"Is he married?" Hyacinth asked.

"No, not at all. He's single. He told me his girlfriend broke up with him on Christmas two years ago," I said.

"Sorry to hear that. He seems like a nice man, Holly," Hannah said. "As we all see, this is a beautiful diner. It seems to have so much history."

"It does. I see what we've been missing," Hollis said, and took a sip of her sweetened iced tea. "Best iced tea I've ever had. Sweetened to perfection."

"It is. I probably drank about three glasses since I've been here," I said with a smile. I looked around and saw Sterling serving drinks to our party guests who were seated at the counter. "The man at the counter? Sterling? He walked *seven miles* in that blizzard to get here."

They all gasped in disbelief!

"Walked? C'mon, Holly. Stop kidding. The storm was way too strong for anyone to walk here in," Hollis said.

"I believe her," Hannah said as she looked sympathetically at Sterling.

"Me too," Hyacinth said. "You wouldn't believe what people have to walk through just to get to work. It took Chris and I and the baby over an hour more than our usual time to get to Mom and Dad's for the party. And we were in a Lambo SUV, a top luxury SUV. That storm was brutal. I couldn't imagine a car breaking down in it, but a person having to walk to get to work in it is incomprehensible, especially on Christmas."

"It is," Hollis said. "It makes me realize just how good of a life I live."

"It should make all of us realize it," Hannah said.

"And it does," I said.

They all nodded in agreement.

"And he has the last name Goode for a reason," I said.

"He sure does," Hannah said with a smile, and drank some of her coffee.

I got up out of my seat.

"Holly, where are you going?" Hyacinth asked.

"ATTENTION, EVERYONE!" I shouted throughout the diner.

Everyone turned their attention to me as it became dead quiet in here.

"I have something I wanna say," I informed them. "First of all, this has been one unexpected Christmas. I never thought I would end up spending my Christmas in a diner, and not only that, my whole family and the party guests would bring the party to me once the roads got cleared up. And I can't thank Rudy and Krista enough for their wonderful hospitality while I've been here, and they have extended this to my family and friends."

Rudy and Krista nodded with a smile.

"And to all of the staff members who came here when you could be celebrating the early hours of this most wonderful day of the year with your family and friends to take care of my family and friends. Thank you so much."

The staff members nodded with a smile.

"And I will not be able to leave here today without thanking Sterling Goode, the man who cleaned out the parking lot so you all would be able to get in here."

"THANK YOU, STERLING!" my friends and family all shouted to him with waves and big smiles.

"You're welcome," Sterling said with a big smile.

"And that's not all about Sterling. I hope you don't mind me saying this, Sterling, because I want my friends and family in here to know."

Sterling looked confused as did almost everyone else. "What is it, Holly?"

I tried to suppress the tears that were welling up in my eyes. "Sterling walked seven miles in that blizzard to get here."

Everyone looked at each other and gasped, and then shut down in silence as the shaking of the heads and sighs began.

"And I wanna make sure he never has to do it again," I pledged. "Hannah, hand me my purse."

Hannah handed my purse to me since they were sitting at the table I was sitting at since I'd been here.

I opened my purse and pulled out my keys to my Bentley Bentayga. "Sterling, I'm giving you my SUV. Merry Christmas."

Everyone gasped in pure shock but in joy at the same time. Rudy and Krista looked at each other and smiled big and they nodded in agreement!

Sterling was so shocked he truly stood stunned. "Holly . . . no. That is too much. This is too much."

"NOTHING IS EVER TOO MUCH FROM MY BABY! GO ON, BABY! YOU KNOW YOU'RE A HARPER!" Dad said with a big smile. My mom nodded as she wiped tears from her eyes, as did all of the women in the diner as the men nodded with big smiles.

I walked over to Sterling and put the keys in his hands as he still stood stunned in the same place; right where he was about to give one of our party guests their appetizers.

Everyone cheered!

"You're excused for the rest of the day, Sterling. Go and enjoy your wonderful gift from Holly. Merry Christmas," Rudy said with a smile, and gave him a hug.

"I feel like I'm dreaming," Sterling said as he wiped tears from his eyes. "The best gift I've ever gotten besides my kids being born. Thank you, Holly. Thank you, Harper family. Y'all are the best. The BEST! I'll be back later on today, Rudy, forget that being excused for the rest of the day!"

We all laughed as he got his coat and we followed along with our phones to get pictures and videos of him with his gift from me. I looked back at the older gentleman as he nodded at me with a smile in recognition and approval for what I'd done, and tended back to his newspaper.

"Well, Holly Harper! No one expected that! That was the nicest thing I think you've ever done for anyone on Christmas!" Hannah said, and ate some more of her collard greens.

"Me giving someone a gift like that is the most I've ever given, but I did it because he deserves it. I couldn't just sit here with a pair of $5,540 freakin' jeweled pants on with a $13,000 coat sitting next to me with the only real fur on it being the collar—and don't get me started on the Birkin. And this man walks in from walking seven miles in a blizzard to get to work here for Christmas? And then plowed the parking lot for you all to make it in here and he didn't even know you all were coming here just as much as I didn't. That was the least I could do."

"It would be the least anyone with a heart could do, Holly," Hyacinth said, and ate some of her fried fish. "This food is delicious, just like you said. Chris and I are definitely gonna have to make coming here a regular for our date nights."

"Willis and I said the same thing," Hannah said with a smile.

"Jack and I already agreed to it," Hollis said.

"If only I can get a husband to agree to it."

They all looked every which way but directly at me as they ate their food.

"Holly, you'll have a husband in due time," Hannah said.

"Yeah," I said, as I looked ahead. I had to do a double take.

To Avery sitting in a booth staring right back at me!

12
THE JOY OF FAMILY

"Holly."

I looked around. "Hey, Vester! How are you?" I asked as we hugged.

"Just fine, Holly. I just wanna tell you personally that was a beautiful thing you did for Sterling Goode. I don't see anyone of your status doing anything like that that often. It definitely needs to be done more."

"I agree. It just broke my heart when I saw him standing there looking like a real-life snowman when he walked in here and Rudy told me he'd walked seven miles to get here just for work. I was still the only one in here besides the older gentleman. I knew right then and there I was giving him my SUV so he would never have to walk here again or anywhere."

"That's why you're a great person, Holly. You can see that joy all over him when you gave him a gift and a gift like that for today. I'm sure he'll remember it for the rest of his life."

"He told me he would," I replied with a smile.

"Oh, and this is my man, Evan," Vester said.

"Nice to meet you, Holly," Evan said.

"Very nice to meet you, too, Evan," I replied with a smile as I looked at Vester.

"Yes, Holly, I'm finally out. I told my parents right before we left to your parents' party that Evan and I are in a serious relationship. They accepted it and us."

I knew it all along, I thought. "Good for you, Vester. Good luck, you two, and Merry Christmas."

"Thank you, Holly, and the same to you," they replied.

I continued on while I stopped and talked to people who said they loved it that the party was moved here and that my parents should make it a tradition. I told them they had to talk to them about that.

I got a tap on my shoulder, and turned around to Avery staring down at me with a smile.

"Hello, Holly," he said with a smile.

"Avery. Haven't seen or talked to you in almost ten years. Ready to apologize?" I asked as I crossed my arms in front of me. "Because legend has it that I'm still in Diamante looking for you."

He grinned. "C'mon, Holly. I'm sorry and felt bad about doing that. I was just so hurt and shocked by your rejection. I haven't done that to any woman since."

"Well, I sure as hell hope you haven't, considering the fact that the woman you left me in the club for to take home with you that night now happens to be your wife." I looked around to find his wife sitting in one of the booths with their two kids as she stared right at me.

He smiled. "Things happen for a reason. And what happened between us that night should not have happened, I admit that. But we weren't an official couple even though everyone thought we should've been by that point. At least I didn't do to you what Caden did to you."

"You were both wrong. Boyfriend or not."

"Yeah, I know we were, Holly. But at least I'm saying I'm sorry now, and I really mean it. I didn't know when I was gonna see you again to tell you in person since this is the first party I've been to in the years since what'd happened between us happened."

"It's done with, Avery. All I wanted was an apology. I've since moved on from it. Merry Christmas."

"Thank you, Holly. Same to you," he said with a smile as he still stared down at me. It was like he still wanted to talk to me even though he was here with his wife and kids. And he didn't even introduce me to them.

I looked over at Rudy as he stared back at me while he put people's plates of food on their tables. "Excuse me." I felt I was officially through with Avery just as I was through with every man who hurt me on this day in the past. I knew we couldn't even be friends anymore. Back then, he wanted something more than I was willing to give him, but he clearly found his joy that night and at my expense, so there was no way I could fully forgive him for it. I walked up to Rudy. "Need any help?"

"No, Holly. You're still a customer here. Krista and I have all the help we need now. Enjoy these first hours of Christmas with your family and friends, and like I said, I feel honored that they brought the party here to you."

"Thank you. But we're just as honored for you to have us here, and I could not have spun out into a better place. I'll never forget it."

"That's great to hear," he replied with a smile.

I sat back down at the table after ordering some more dessert while I looked through my phone as texts along with pictures came flooding in with the typical Merry Christmas wishes, but this Christmas was far from typical. I picked up my mug and took a sip of my coffee as I continued to have a look-see . . . and almost spit out my coffee when I saw one from Caden!

Merry Christmas, Holly. I hope we can talk soon.

I hadn't heard from him in the seven years since he decided to propose to someone else with a 7-carat diamond ring, but decided to give me that fancy mug as if it was gonna make up for it. I sighed because I didn't know whether or not I actually wanted to respond to him. I held up the exact mug he'd given me and took a picture of myself with a cheesy, sarcastic smile:

Caden. Haven't heard from you in seven years. Cheers.

I waited for him to respond.

Wow, Holly. I didn't think you were ever gonna respond to me. You look great! And you bought another one of those mugs, huh? I guess I didn't break you after all. No pun intended.

No, you didn't, and none taken. And you look like shit! Merry Christmas, prick!

I turned off my phone and continued to eat another round of dessert, but this time I opted for the banana pudding. "I'm gonna go talk to Krista," I told Hyacinth since she was the only sitting at the table right now with her baby.

"Okay. *I can't believe* she's Marwell's wife!"

"Yeah, I couldn't believe it when she told me, too. But she is, and I know why. I'll be right back."

"Holly," Rudy said.

"Yes?"

"Can you go get Krista for me?"

"Sure. I was just going back there to talk to her."

"Okay."

I went into the back where Krista was busy at cooking along with ten others for my family and our party guests. I couldn't believe how busy it'd gotten so fast and how fast these staff members got here. "Krista?"

"Yes, Holly?" she asked with a smile.

"Rudy says he needs you out front for something."

"Okay," she replied with a smile, and had another cook take over what she was cooking.

"You have the most amazing family," Krista said with a smile. "It's an honor to me that they brought their party here."

"Rudy said the same thing, and I thank the both of you because it's an honor for us to all be here," I said with a smile.

We walked out to the front . . . and Krista gasped!

"Merry Christmas, Krista," *Marwell said!*

"DADDY!" their kids said as they ran up to him and hugged him while two lawyers stood by his side and smiled.

Krista cried as she walked over to him and they embraced as well. Everyone had their phones up getting their own personal footage of this, as the women wiped tears from their eyes. "What? My goodness! You never told me you were coming home today!"

"I wanted it to be a surprise," he said with a smile as his kids still clung to him. "I knew this would happen for weeks now. My partner finally admitted he had everything to do with everything, and provided the proof about setting me up. I guess some people really do have a conscience."

"They do," Krista said with a smile. They embraced with a kiss once again.

"And I can't believe the entire Harper family is in here with their party guests! WOW!" Marwell said as he looked around.

We all laughed as Marwell and I locked eyes with each other.

"Holly Harper. It's been a while since the last time we've seen each other. How are you?"

"I'm great, Marwell. Just great. How are you?"

"I'm the happiest I've been in years."

We hugged while I could see that everyone's phones were on us now. I could tell he was still in his prison uniform. I looked at Rudy as he continued to smile at me.

"You chose the right woman to marry. Krista is a wonderful woman."

"Thank you, Holly," Krista said with a smile.

"Yes, thank you," Marwell said.

"It's on us if you wanna stay and eat, Marwell," my dad said with a smile. I remembered that he liked Marwell the most out of all of my boyfriends.

"Thank you, Mr. Harper," Marwell said with a smile.

"I'll cook your favorite. Come on in the back," Krista said.

"I look forward to it," Marwell replied with a big smile. He held the hands of their kids as they walked into the back, and their lawyers stayed out here and mingled with my family.

I smiled as I watched them. I was truly happy that he was out of prison, and I knew they had a long road ahead of them to get things back to how they once were, and I would be supporting them all the way.

Rudy came out with his phone. “Yeah, you gotta see this to believe it. I told you the entire Harper family was here! And it was Holly Harper who was here first. MY PARENTS WANNA SAY HI FROM JAMAICA!” he informed all of us and pointed his phone towards us.

“HI!” We all said as we waved with smiles. “MERRY CHRISTMAS!”

“And I wanna discuss possible expansion opportunities with you all. This food is too good to have in only one place. I’m giving Rudy my card right now,” Dad said to Rudy’s parents, and then handed his card to Rudy.

“Thank you, Mr. Harper,” Rudy said with a smile. He looked at me.

I smiled with a nod.

Several minutes later, Marwell and Krista came back out to the front and talked to everyone.

I got a tap on my shoulder.

“Can I talk to you alone for a few minutes?” Rudy asked me.

“Sure,” I said with a smile. I looked back and noticed everyone having such a great time here in these early morning Christmas hours. This was definitely better than the party at my parents’ house. I looked at the end of the counter and noticed that the older gentleman had left. I didn’t even see him leave.

We walked into his office.

“I can’t thank you enough for all of this, Rudy.”

“I’m not the one you should thank.”

“What?”

“You should thank yourself,” he said with a smile. “All of this happened because of you.”

“And it will be a Christmas I will never forget.”

“Me too.”

We continued to stare at each other.

“Um . . . and I wanted to know if I could see you again after today?”

I didn’t know why I was surprised that he’d asked me this, but I was. “Sure, I would love that.”

"You brought so much joy to me and my family today, and words can't even express how much joy you brought to Sterling."

"And I want many more joyous moments."

"And so do I," he said with a smile.

"This is the first Christmas in years that I feel some true joy on. And I meet a man whose last name is Joy. Can't make this up."

"No, you can't. Hopefully we'll have lots of joy in the future."

I smiled. "I hope so."

I felt a kissing moment coming on as he continued to stare at me, but knew he probably didn't wanna ruin this moment between us.

"Well, let me get back out there. This has definitely been the busiest Christmas I can ever remember with it being just a few hours into the day, and definitely the best," he said.

"I agree, and thank you."

He gave me a soft kiss on my forehead.

I smiled big because I wanted his beautiful lips to kiss some part of my face, I couldn't lie! "Did the older gentleman tell you he was leaving?" I decided to ask so the kiss wouldn't turn into something a lot more and especially back here.

"What older gentleman?"

"The older gentleman who was sitting at the end of the counter reading the newspaper and smoking all night."

He gave me a look of total confusion. "Holly, there was no one sitting at the end of the counter the whole night."

I gasped in shock. "Okay, stop playing with me, Rudy. There was an older gentleman sitting at the end of the counter when I first walked in here. He was the only one sitting in here. He stayed here until a few minutes ago. We never spoke, but he would smile at me and nod once in a while."

"What did he look like?"

"My Mark Roberts drummer figurine I got just weeks ago. See." I pulled up a picture of my 17-inch figurine on my phone for him to see.

"Wow, he's beautiful," he said with a smile. He then pulled up a picture on his phone. "Are you talking about him?"

He showed me a picture of the man I saw sitting at the end of the counter. He was sitting in the exact spot doing his thing, but the picture looked very old.

"YES!"

"That's Rudolph Joy the First. My grandfather. He's the one who opened this restaurant; the one who started it all. He died 50 years ago, Holly."

I gasped in complete and total shock! "That was him, Rudy! Oh my god! That was him!"

He smiled. "Other people have told me that they've seen him sitting at the end of the counter doing exactly what you said he was doing—smoking and reading the newspaper. Unfortunately, that smoking is what killed him; there was nothing the doctors could do for him. Like you, people who have seen him told me they've seen him mainly around this time of the year. He loved Christmas just like everyone else."

Tears welled up in my eyes. "Wow, I never thought I would have that powerful something like seeing people who aren't here anymore."

"Yeah, not everyone has it. I don't have it. I wasn't even born yet when he passed. My grandmother passed over 30 years ago, but no one has seen her here, just him since he was here a lot more than her since she was still taking care of the family."

I smiled as tears flowed down from my eyes as he wiped them away. I was glad I was wearing waterproof makeup. "Like I said and have been saying since I've been here, this will definitely be a Christmas I will never ever forget. Never ever."

"And I like I said, me too."

We hugged.

"Let's get back out there to everyone," he suggested with a smile.

"Okay," I replied with a smile.

We walked back out to where everyone was.

"This is what we play at our party every Christmas since it's been out," Dad said, and put some change in the beautiful jukebox, and Aretha Franklin's "Joy to the World" turned on!

And we all clapped and cheered as we turned this diner into a church as we all danced all over it and sang to the song because it was by far a Christmas party favorite. I smiled as Rudy and I danced with each other, and I'd hope this was the start of something beautiful between the two of us. My favorite time of the year had been restored with the joy that I could only get from family and real friends and from giving, and there was nowhere else I wanted to be right now for a Christmas that my family and friends, nor I, will ever forget.

HOLLY and RUDY
COMING SOON

ABOUT THE AUTHOR

Sheila Murdock is a combination of her birth name and her late grandmother's maiden name on her mother's side.

When she's not writing, she enjoys watching movies and TV shows—old and new—on YouTube, Netflix, and Amazon Prime Video, but always loves a surprising show she can find on cable TV. She also enjoys reading all kinds of non-fiction, but has a particular interest in African-American historical and contemporary non-fiction, but will read an occasional fiction book. She enjoys listening to old-school/throwback rap, hip-hop, and R&B, and jazz music from any era.